Elodie
the Lamb
Fairy

by Daisy Meadows

ORCHARD

www.rainbowmagic.co.uk

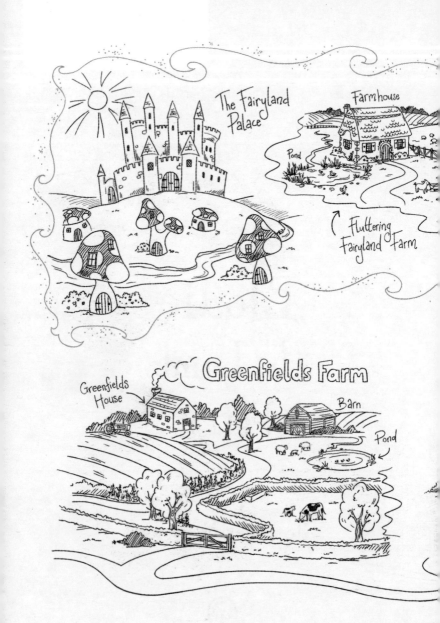

Jack Frost's Spell

I want a farm that's just for me,
With animals I won't set free.
It's far too slow to seek each one.
Let fairy magic get this done!

With magic from the fairy farm,
I'll grant my wish – to their alarm!
And if I spoil the humans' fun,
Then Jack Frost really will have won!

Contents

Alarm on the Farm

COCK-A-DOODLE-DOO!

Kirsty Tate and Rachel Walker sat up in bed at exactly the same moment. For a few seconds, they couldn't think where they were. Then they remembered, and shared an excited smile.

"You know you're on a farm when a cockerel is your alarm clock," said

Rachel, bouncing out of bed. "Quick, let's get dressed. I can't wait to say good morning to all the animals."

This was their first full day at Greenfields Farm, just outside Wetherbury, where they were going to spend the whole of the spring half term. The farm was owned by Harriet and Niall Hawkins, friends of Kirsty's parents, and they were getting ready to open it up to paying visitors at the end of the week. The Tates and Rachel had come to help them.

Kirsty slipped out of bed too, and threw open the yellow curtains. The walls of the farmhouse were so thick that the windowsill was big enough to sit on. Kirsty put the blanket from her bed on the sill, and then perched there, gazing out over the farm. She could see the barn where they had met Blossom the cow, and the trees that hid the sparkling duck pond. Over to the left she could see a green pasture, with sheep dotted around it like little puffs of cotton wool.

"It's going to be a lovely sunny day," said Rachel, joining her at the window. "This is perfect weather for working outside."

"I wouldn't mind rain or snow, as long as we get to spend the day with baby animals," said Kirsty with a smile.

The day before, the Hawkinses had asked the girls to look after the baby animals on the farm. Rachel and Kirsty were thrilled. They both loved animals, and they usually found that animals loved them too.

As soon as the girls were dressed and their beds were made, they hurried down the creaky farmhouse stairs to the big kitchen. Niall and Harriet Hawkins were already there with the Tates.

"Good morning, you two," said Niall in

a cheerful voice. "You're just in time for a big Greenfields Farm breakfast. Eggs freshly laid this morning, milk and butter from Blossom the cow, and hot, crusty bread straight out of the oven."

"It sounds delicious," said Kirsty, her stomach rumbling.

As the girls tucked in to their food, Harriet went through her list of what needed to be done that day. She asked Mr and Mrs Tate to finish painting the welcome centre, and then smiled at the girls.

"I've got a very special job for you to do this morning," she said. "Five lambs have been born here recently, and we want to get them used to bottle-feeding. The visitors will love being able to feed

lambs. Will you go to the sheep pasture after breakfast and bottle-feed the lambs?"

"We'd love to," said Rachel at once. "What a perfect way to start the day."

"Would you like me to come with you and show you how to do it?" Niall asked.

Rachel and Kirsty shook their heads.

"No, thank you," said Kirsty. "We've both bottle-fed lambs before. I'm sure we'll remember what to do."

"That's wonderful," said Harriet. "Thank you, Rachel and Kirsty."

"Thank you for letting us do it," said Rachel, smiling. "I love lambs – they're so soft and woolly. They're my favourite animal babies."

Kirsty laughed and squeezed her best friend's hand.

"You say that about all the animal babies," she told her.

"I know," said Rachel, also laughing. "I can never make up my mind. They're all so cute."

The girls had two fresh speckled eggs each, followed by toast, butter and home-made blackberry jam. They washed it all down with glasses of creamy, frothy milk, and then carried their plates to the sink.

"Thank you," said Harriet. "We'll finish tidying up in here. I've put a bucket of bottles next to the back door for the

lambs. Do you know where the sheep
pasture is?"

"Yes," said Kirsty. "We saw it from our
bedroom window this morning."

"The lambs are in a pen beside the
pasture," said Harriet. "See you later,
girls."

Rachel and
Kirsty pulled on
their wellies
and then
Rachel
picked up
the bucket
of bottles.
They said
goodbye to
the grown-
ups and headed out towards the pasture.

To get there, they had to pass the barn. Blossom was outside, and she let out a happy moo as they walked past.

"Good morning, Blossom," said Rachel, going over to her and patting her side.

"We can't stop. We've got an important job to do this morning."

She held up the bucket of bottles, and Blossom mooed again.

"Yes, it's milk," said Kirsty. "See you later on, Blossom. We've got some animal babies to feed!"

Baa-Miaow

The girls walked side by side up the path towards the sheep pasture. The morning breeze carried the fresh scent of grass to them, and they took deep breaths to drink it in.

"I wish I could live here," said Kirsty. "I love the countryside."

Rachel didn't reply. She was peering at something on the wooden pasture fence. It was an animal, and it was stepping carefully along the top of the fence.

"What *is* that?" she asked.

"A cat?" said Kirsty, sounding unsure.

"It looks too big for a cat," Rachel said.

They sped up, and as they got closer they went even faster. They could now see what the animal was, but neither of them could quite believe what was in front of their eyes.

"It's a lamb," said Kirsty in wonder. "I've never seen a lamb balancing on a fence before."

"I've never heard a lamb saying 'miaow' either," said Rachel, frowning. "Listen."

As they got closer, Kirsty heard it too. The lamb was miaowing like a cat. The girls exchanged a worried glance.

"Jack Frost and his goblins are causing trouble again," said Kirsty. "I suppose we should have expected it after what happened yesterday."

23

The girls thought back to their adventures of the day before. They had been watching the new little ducklings on the Greenfields Farm pond, when Debbie the Duckling Fairy had fluttered out of a duck's nest. Rachel and Kirsty were used to finding fairies in unexpected places, so they were excited to meet her. They had been friends of Fairyland ever since they had met the Rainbow Fairies on Rainspell Island. They had been best friends since that day too.

Debbie had taken them to see the animals at Fluttering Fairyland Farm, a magical farm that hovered in mid-air among the fluffy white clouds of Fairyland. There, the girls had met the other Baby Farm Animal Fairies – Elodie the Lamb Fairy, Penelope the Foal Fairy and Billie the Baby Goat Fairy. They had also seen the magical baby farm animals who helped the fairies to look after baby farm animals everywhere. It had been one of the most amazing visits to Fairyland that Rachel and Kirsty could remember. But then Jack Frost had turned up with three of his mischievous goblins, and everything had gone terribly wrong.

Jack Frost wanted some cute, cuddly animals to make his own petting zoo at the Ice Castle. So far, he only had his snow goose and her baby, Snowdrop, and he wanted more. So he and his goblins had stolen the fairies' magical farm animals.

At once, Debbie had whisked the girls back to Greenfields Farm, where they found that things were already going wrong. The ducklings were acting like puppies, along with Splashy, Debbie's magical duckling.

Thinking about their adventures the day before, Rachel and Kirsty stared at the miaowing lamb.

"Jack Frost has done this," said Kirsty in a worried voice.
"Do you think all the lambs on the farm are acting like cats?"

"It might be all the lambs in the human world," Rachel replied.

"What will the Hawkinses say if they

come to see the lambs and find them like this?" said Kirsty.

"We helped Debbie get Splashy back from the goblin who stole her and all the ducklings went back to normal," said Rachel. "We have to get Elodie's magical lamb back – then all the other lambs will be themselves again."

"We have to get *all* the missing magical animals back," said Kirsty. "Without them, Greenfields Farm will never be ready for visitors, and farm babies will be changed forever."

"You're right," said Rachel. "But first, let's get that lamb down from the fence."

Big Green Wellies

Rachel put the bucket of bottles down.
Then, moving slowly and quietly, the girls
tiptoed up to the lamb.

"Hello," said Rachel in a gentle voice.
"What are you doing up here?"

She ran her hand along the lamb's
back. It opened its little mouth, but
instead of a bleat, it let out a loud purr.

"I wonder if it will let me pick it up," said Kirsty.

She tried to put her arms around it, but the lamb leapt down from the fence and scampered off. It moved more like a cat than a lamb.

"Should we follow it?" Rachel said.

"No, wait," said Kirsty. "Look…"

She was staring at a little tuft of lamb's-wool that was caught on the fence. Rachel looked too, and saw that the

wool had a faint glow about it. The glow
grew stronger and brighter, and then the
tuft of wool opened out like a flower.
There was a little burst of silver sparkles,
and then Elodie the Lamb Fairy was
sitting in the middle of
the wool with her
legs curled up
underneath
her. She was
wearing a
soft pink
dress edged
with purple
detailing, and
a fluffy lamb's-wool
waistcoat. She clapped her hands when
she saw the girls, and her brown curls
bounced merrily up and down.

"I found you," she said with a smile.
"Debbie told me how you helped her
find Splashy. It's wonderful to have him
back at Fluttering
Fairyland Farm.
Will you help
me to find
Fluffy so that
I can take
her home
too?"

"We're always happy to help our fairy
friends," said Rachel. "Oh, Elodie, you've
come at just the right moment. We've just
seen a lamb acting like a cat."

"That doesn't sound good," said Elodie.
"Right now I don't think *any* of the
lambs in the human world will be feeling
normal. Where can the goblin be hiding

Fluffy? As soon as I get her back home, all other lambs will start acting like lambs again."

"We'll help you look as soon as we've fed the other lambs," said Kirsty.

She picked up the bucket of bottles and Elodie fluttered inside it to hide. Then Rachel and Kirsty hurried up to the lambs' pen. But when they got there, just one lamb 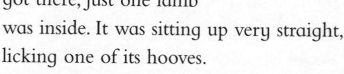 was inside. It was sitting up very straight, licking one of its hooves.

"Hello," said Rachel, stepping inside the pen. "Where are your friends, little lamb?

Where have they all gone?"

The lamb stood up, stretched, and then rubbed its face against Rachel's legs, just like a cat rubbing its whiskers. It started to purr, and when Kirsty came into the pen it pressed against her legs too. Then it weaved around both girls in a figure of eight, still purring loudly.

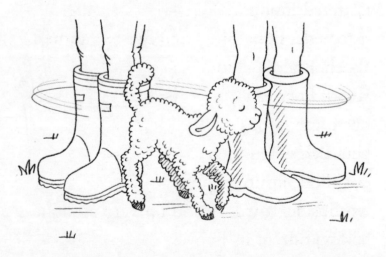

"You know, the goblins don't have very much imagination," said Rachel. "The one who took Splashy came here, and I bet the other two came here too."

"I've got an idea," said Kirsty. "Elodie, if you turn us into fairies, we could fly over the farm to look for Fluffy and the other lambs. We'll be able to search a lot more quickly that way."

Elodie popped out of the bucket and glanced around. There were no other people in sight. She lifted her wand and did a little twirl in mid-air. Instantly, the girls felt themselves whirling around as they shrank to fairy size, and delicate wings unfurled on their backs.

They were scooped up on magical puffy
clouds and swept into the air. The little
lamb rose up on to her hind
legs to watch them.
She batted at
them with
her front
hoof, but
the little
clouds
whisked
them out of
reach. Then the
clouds melted away
and Elodie came darting after them.
Together, they zoomed up over the sheep
pasture.

"Look down there," said Rachel. "The
lambs are in the pasture."

Now that they had a good view, they could see four lambs in the pasture. Two of them were rolling around together, play-fighting. Another lamb was busy chasing a leaf that was dancing in the breeze, pouncing and freeing it over and over again. The fourth lamb was scratching at the newly painted fence.

"It's just what we were afraid of," said Kirsty. "They're all acting like cats."

The lambs were miaowing so loudly that the fairies could hear them clearly, even from high above. The sheep in the pasture were staying away from the lambs, and giving them some very confused looks. When the leaf-chasing lamb got too close, one of the sheep let out a loud, grumpy baa.

The lambs were startled by the loud
noise. They all leapt up on to the pasture
fence, balanced there for a moment, and
then jumped down and ran off towards
the farm.

"Oh no," said Kirsty. "How are we
going to get them back?"

She and Elodie watched in a panic
as the lambs scattered. Rachel was still
looking all around, hoping to be lucky
enough to spot Fluffy. There was no
magical lamb in sight, but there was
someone down in a grove of trees at the
bottom of the pasture. He was wearing
bright green dungarees
and wellies, and he
was looking up
into a tree.

"Who is that?" Rachel asked. "It doesn't look like Niall. Are there any other people working on the farm this week, Kirsty?"

Kirsty looked where Rachel was pointing, and her mouth fell open.

"That's not a grown-up," she said. "It's not even a human. Look at his enormous wellies. That's a goblin!"

Following the Trail

The goblin seemed to be calling to someone in the tree.

"Come on," said Elodie. "Let's go and find out what he's doing. He's one of Jack Frost's goblins, so I'll bet you anything he's up to mischief."

Rachel, Kirsty and Elodie flew down towards the grove of trees. As they got closer, they saw a magical glow through the leaves.

"There's something in the tree," said Kirsty. "Oh, Elodie, I think it's Fluffy!"

The magical little lamb was balancing on a low branch. She looked alone and confused.

"Fluffy!" Elodie called.

Fluffy was startled, and she jumped down from the branch in a panic. She landed in the goblin's arms, and he gave a loud squawk of delight.

44

"You *do* want to cuddle me," he said. "You're so soft and sweet. I want more cuddles. I want *all* the cuddles!"

He squeezed her so tightly that she started to squirm and wriggle in his arms.

Seconds later, she twisted away from him and dashed away.

"Come back!" he shouted.

"Fluffy!" Elodie cried out.

The goblin charged after the little lamb, stumbling with every step he took in his massive wellies. Fluffy pressed her belly to the grass and crawled under the shrubbery behind the grove of trees.

"We have to follow her," said Rachel, zooming into the greenery.

Elodie and Kirsty flew after her, but by the time they caught up, Fluffy had completely disappeared. They heard the goblin crashing into the bushes behind them.

Kirsty and Rachel looked at each other in dismay. How were they going to get Fluffy back now?

Rachel looked around and spotted a few tufts of Fluffy's wool clinging to the undergrowth.

"A trail," she said. "Maybe we can follow it. It might lead us to Fluffy, just like the breadcrumbs in the story *Hansel and Gretel.*"

"That's a brilliant idea," said Elodie, clapping her hands together. "Quickly, there's not a moment to lose. We can't let Fluffy disappear again."

Staying low and flitting through the
undergrowth, the fairies hunted for
the little wisps of glowing white wool.

Here and there they found them clinging
to twigs and caught on thorns. Rachel
picked up each piece and held them all
in her hand. The trail led them through
the shrubbery, over to a bush, and when
they peered underneath it they saw Fluffy
curled up like a cat.

Elodie put her finger to her lips, and
they all backed away from the bush.

"We have to be very careful," she
whispered. "Now we've found her, we
mustn't frighten her away again."

"Maybe she would come with us if we
had a cat toy," said Kirsty, remembering
that they had used a toy to help them get
Splashy the duckling back.

Rachel looked down at the tufts of
Fluffy's glowing woolly coat in her hand.

49

"Wool," she said. "Cats love balls of wool – they will chase them for hours. Could you make a ball of wool, Elodie?"

Elodie flicked her wand, and instantly Rachel was holding a large ball of soft blue wool.

"Perfect," said Rachel. "We will need to be human for this."

With another wave of her wand, Elodie turned the girls back into humans once again.

"This shrubbery suddenly seems a lot

more cramped," said Kirsty with a quiet laugh. "OK, Rachel, I'm ready. It's time to get Fluffy."

Chase!

Kneeling down, Rachel rolled the ball of wool towards the little lamb, keeping hold of one end of the wool. The ball nudged up against Fluffy's nose and she opened one eye. Kirsty and Rachel crossed their fingers. But Fluffy just closed her eye again. Rachel pulled the ball of wool back towards herself.

"Let me try," said Kirsty.

She rolled the wool and it bumped up against Fluffy's hoof. Again, one of her eyes flickered for a moment. But she was just not interested. Kirsty pulled the wool back towards herself again.

The girls heard a rustling sound behind them, and turned around as a pair of green hands parted two bushes. The goblin peered at them through the shrubbery.

"What are you doing here?" he snapped.

He was glaring at Elodie – he hadn't noticed Fluffy under the bush. Trying to look casual, Rachel edged sideways so that she was in front of the bush. The goblin looked at the ball of wool.

"I'll have that," he said, reaching out and snatching it out of Kirsty's hands. "I need it so I can take the lamb to Jack Frost's petting zoo at the Ice Castle."

"You can't just take things that don't belong to you," said Kirsty, pulling the wool back.

"Give it to me!" the goblin squawked.

He scrabbled towards her, and Kirsty jumped up and ran away, out of the grove of trees and towards the sheep pasture. Rachel glanced at Fluffy, and noticed that the little lamb had opened her eyes. She had half raised her head, pricking up her ears.

"She's interested in the chase," Rachel said to Elodie, then cupped her hands around her mouth to call in a loud voice, "Kirsty, drop the end of the wool!"

Kirsty didn't know why Rachel wanted her to drop the end of the wool, but she trusted her best friend, so as she was running she unwound some of the

wool and let it trail along the ground
behind her. The goblin, who was already
stumbling in his big wellies, now tripped
over the end of the wool.

"Stop!" he screeched crossly. "Give me
that wool!"

He scrambled up again and carried
on running. Kirsty zigzagged around the
bottom of the pasture, getting closer and
closer to the shrubbery. Then, as fast as
lightning, Fluffy suddenly darted out and
pounced on the end of the wool with a
loud miaow.

While Fluffy was busy patting the wool
with her hoof, Rachel rushed forward
and put her arms around the little lamb.

Elodie fluttered down and placed one hand on Fluffy's back. Immediately, Fluffy shrank to fairy size and let out a loud baa.

"Hurray!" Kirsty cheered, throwing her arms around Rachel. "Thank goodness she's a lamb again."

The goblin sank down on the grass and rubbed his eyes.

"I only wanted to cuddle her and feel her soft wool," he said in a sad voice. "She's so sweet."

Elodie's face softened as she looked at the goblin. Rachel and Kirsty could tell that she felt sorry for him.

"There are other ways to enjoy the feel of a lamb's wool," said the little fairy in a gentle voice.

She waved her wand and a jumper appeared on the goblin's knee. It was bright green, and it looked as fluffy as a lamb. The goblin picked it up and pressed it against his cheek.

"This is the softest thing I've ever felt," he said.

He cuddled it and stroked it against his other cheek.

A big smile spread across his face.

"It's for you to keep," said Elodie.

The goblin jumped up and skipped away across the pasture.

"We should go back to the lambs' pen," said Kirsty. "Now that Fluffy is back with Elodie, all the little lambs should be back to normal."

"Let's go and find out," said Rachel.

The Magic of the Farm

The girls raced across the pasture to the pen, with Elodie zooming along in the air behind them. But when they reached the pen, they saw that there was still only one little lamb inside.

"At least he is behaving like a lamb again," said Rachel, watching him springing around the pen.

The girls stepped into the pen and
the lamb trotted over to them, bleating
with happiness. They stroked him and he
nuzzled them both.

"The other lambs must still be
wandering around the farm," said Kirsty.
"How are we going to find them and get
them to come back here?"

"I don't know," said Kirsty, "but we *have* to find them. They are going to be one of the biggest attractions here on the farm."

"I'll use my magic," said Elodie. "Now that Fluffy is back with me, I will be able to bring the lambs back easily."

But just as she raised her wand, they all heard a high-pitched whistle coming from the direction of the farmhouse. They raised their hands to  shade their eyes from the sun, and saw Harriet standing outside the barn. She blew her whistle again.

"What is she doing?" Rachel asked.

Just then, Patch the sheepdog appeared around the side of the barn, and in front of him were four white lambs. Elodie laughed in delight.

"I'll let the sheepdog sort out the lambs," she said. "It's time for me to take Fluffy back to the Fluttering Fairyland Farm."

She hovered beside Kirsty, and dropped

a kiss on her cheek. Fluffy nuzzled
against her human friend too. Then they
did the same to Rachel.

"Thank you both
for helping me to find
Fluffy," Elodie said. "You're
wonderful. Without you, she
would still be miaowing
and purring."

"We're just happy
that she's back where
she belongs," said
Kirsty.

Elodie smiled, and then she and Fluffy
disappeared in a puff of silvery sparkles.
Patch was just guiding the lambs up the
path, led by Harriet. Now that they were
closer, Rachel and Kirsty could hear the
lambs baaing in shrill voices.

67

Harriet opened the lambs' pen, and then Patch moved the lambs into it. He ran left and right, keeping low to the ground. His glossy black-and-white coat gleamed in the sunshine.

The last lamb skittered into the pen and Harriet closed the gate. Rachel and Kirsty hurried up to her.

"We're really sorry," said Kirsty at once.

68

"We were supposed to be taking care of the lambs, but they were already out of the pen when we arrived to feed them."

"Don't worry," said Harriet. "Patch has a magic touch with lambs. I can't imagine how they got out of the pen, though. It's not as if they could have jumped over the fence!"

Kirsty and Rachel shared a secret smile. What would Harriet have said if she had seen the lambs earlier?

They took a bottle each from the bucket, and went into the pen. They knelt down and waited for the curious little lambs to come closer. Then they offered the bottles. Soon the girls were feeding the first two lambs, cuddling their soft, woolly coats as they drank their milk.

"Well," said Harriet with a laugh. "It looks as if you two have got a magic touch with the lambs as well. Come on, Patch. Let's leave Rachel and Kirsty to feed the lambs in peace."

As Harriet and Patch walked away, the girls exchanged happy smiles.

"Feeding baby lambs has to be one of the best feelings in the whole world," said Rachel. "I love them so much."

"Me too," said Kirsty. "I just hope that we can help the two other Baby Farm Animal Fairies to get their magical animals back by the time Greenfields Farm opens for visitors."

"Everyone should have the chance to know the magic of caring for animals," said Rachel, smiling down at the little lamb she was feeding. "The fairies need us, and we won't let them down. I can't wait for our next magical adventure!"

The End

**Now it's time for Kirsty and
Rachel to help...**

Penelope the Foal Fairy

Read on for a sneak peek...

"Just one day left until the farm's grand opening," said Kirsty Tate.

She was peering at a computer screen over the shoulders of Harriet and Niall Hawkins, the owners of Greenfields Farm. Her parents, Mr and Mrs Tate, and her best friend, Rachel Walker, were also gazing at the computer. They were all looking at the design for the new poster to advertise the farm.

"I feel jumpy with excitement every time I think about the grand opening tomorrow," said Rachel.

"I feel jumpy with *nervousness* every

time I think about it," said Harriet with a laugh. "I can't believe there's just one day left."

"I'm sure everything will be fine," said Mr Tate, patting Harriet's shoulder.

The Tates and Rachel were all spending spring half term at Greenfields Farm, just outside Wetherbury. The Tates were friends with Harriet and Niall, and they had all been helping to get the farm ready. Tomorrow, Greenfields Farm would open to visitors for the first time, complete with a children's petting farm.

"You've all been wonderful," said Niall, half turning in his chair to smile up at them. "Especially you, Rachel and Kirsty. We were worried about being too busy to look after the baby animals this week, but you've done everything for them."

"It's been a treat to look after them,"

said Kirsty with a smile. Mr Tate was still gazing at the poster design.

"I think it needs more photos of the farm," he said.

Read **Penelope the Foal Fairy** to find out
what adventures are in store for Kirsty and Rachel!

Competition!

The Baby Animal Farm Fairies have created
a special competition just for you!

Collect all four books in the Baby Animal Farm series
and answer the special questions in the back of each one.

**Jack Frost's snow
goose's baby is called**

_ _ _ _ _ _ _ _ _

Once you have all four answers, take the first letter from
each one and arrange them to spell a secret word!
When you have the answer, go online and enter!

We will put all the correct entries into a draw and select
a winner to receive a special Rainbow Magic Goody Bag
featuring lots of treats for you and your fairy friends.
The winner will also feature in a new Rainbow Magic story!

Enter online now at www.rainbowmagicbooks.co.uk

No purchase required. Only one entry per child.
One prize draw will take place on 30/06/2017 and two winners will be chosen.
Alternatively UK readers can send the answer on a postcard to: Rainbow Magic,
The Baby Animal Farm Fairies Competition, Orchard Books, Carmelite House,
50 Victoria Embankment, London, EC4Y 0DZ.
Australian readers can write to: Rainbow Magic, The Baby Animal Farm Fairies Competition,
Hachette Children's Books, Level 17/207 Kent St, Sydney, NSW 2000.
E-mail: childrens.books@hachette.com.au.
New Zealand readers should write to: Rainbow Magic, The Baby Animal Farm
Fairies Competition, PO Box 3255, Shortland St, Auckland 1140

Calling all parents, carers and teachers!
The Rainbow Magic fairies are here to help
your child enter the magical world of reading.
Whatever reading stage they are at, there's
a Rainbow Magic book for everyone!
Here is Lydia the Reading Fairy's guide to
supporting your child's journey at all levels.

1

Starting Out

Our Rainbow Magic Beginner Readers are perfect for first-time readers who are just beginning to develop reading skills and confidence. Approved by teachers, they contain a full range of educational levelling, as well as lively full-colour illustrations.

2

Developing Readers

Rainbow Magic Early Readers contain longer stories and wider vocabulary for building stamina and growing confidence. These are adaptations of our most popular Rainbow Magic stories, specially developed for younger readers in conjunction with an Early Years reading consultant, with full-colour illustrations.

3

Going Solo

The Rainbow Magic chapter books - a mixture of series and one-off specials - contain accessible writing to encourage your child to venture into reading independently. These highly collectible and much-loved magical stories inspire a love of reading to last a lifetime.

www.rainbowmagicbooks.co.uk

"Rainbow Magic got my daughter reading chapter books. Great sparkly covers, cute fairies and traditional stories full of magic that she found impossible to put down" - Mother of Edie (6 years)

"Florence LOVES the Rainbow Magic books. She really enjoys reading now" - Mother of Florence (6 years)

The Rainbow Magic Reading Challenge

Well done, fairy friend – you have completed the book!
This book was worth 5 points.

See how far you have climbed on the
Reading Rainbow opposite.

The more books you read, the more points you will get,
and the closer you will be to becoming a Fairy Princess!

How to get your Reading Rainbow
1. Cut out the coin below
2. Go to the Rainbow Magic website
3. Download and print out your poster
4. Add your coin and climb up the Reading Rainbow!

There's all this and lots more at
www.rainbowmagicbooks.co.uk

You'll find activities, competitions, stories, a special
newsletter and complete profiles of all the
Rainbow Magic fairies. Find a fairy with your name!